A MAGNOLIA KISS

THE RED STILETTO BOOK CLUB SERIES

ANNE-MARIE MEYER

For My Daughter

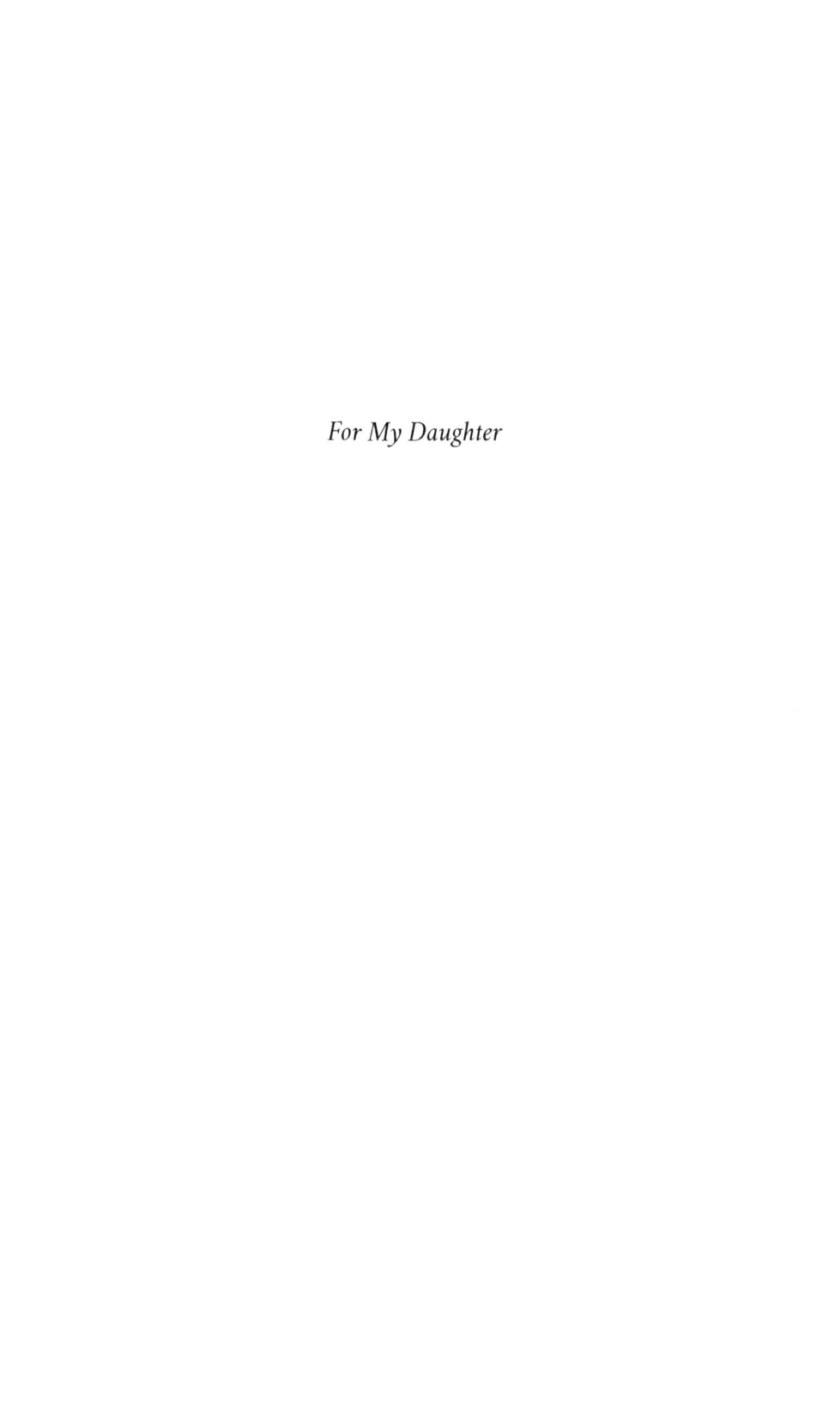

1

SCARLETT

"So, you'll be gone from tonight until Monday?" Maggie asked as she followed after me. We were across the bridge, in Newport, at a grocery store to get fixings for some new gelato flavors I wanted to try out. Since Maggie needed to pick up an order of sheets, we'd decided to make it a group outing that included a quick stop at Macy's Seafood Bar and Grill for lunch.

It was a perfect July day with the breeze coming off the ocean and filling my nose with the sweet smell of water and salt. The sun was warm, and it beat down on my shoulders as we grabbed a cart and wheeled it through the sliding doors of Mom and Pop's Grocery.

Ice-cold air conditioning hit me, causing me to shiver. I tightened my grip around the shopping cart handle and tucked my arms in tighter to my chest. Maggie wandered over to the oranges and I followed her.

"Yep. To participate in the challenge, you have to dedicate the entire weekend to the pier. I've already got my spot marked off, and it's the primo spot." I brought my fingers to my lips and kissed them like an Italian chef would do when they created the perfect pasta dish.

Maggie chuckled as she filled a plastic bag with oranges. "Well, I'm excited for you. I hope you win."

I nodded. Not only would I receive the coveted Magnolia fishing trophy—which had been the wish of my grandfather who passed away four years ago—but I would also win five thousand dollars. Which, for my struggling gelato shack, would mean a lot. I didn't want to admit it, but there was a small chance that I might have to close the little shop's doors at the end of the season.

I didn't want to—it was a legacy my grandmother left me—but if I couldn't get sales up and steady, I would have to turn over the keys to the bank.

I sighed as Maggie and I walked through the store. I grabbed a frozen bag of cherries for a rum black cherry flavor I wanted to test out plus a giant bottle of multi-colored sprinkles for a confetti cake flavor. Once my cart was full of what I needed, we checked out and climbed back into my 1986 Chevy pickup.

When I turned the key, the engine roared to life.

Maggie and I chatted all the way back to Magnolia Inn. She was excited because, this weekend, the inn was completely booked for the first time since she opened a few months ago. She and Archer had been working nonstop to bring the inn back to its former glory. They needed it to work if they were going to prove to Maggie's mom—the owner of the inn—that it was more profitable to keep the inn than it would be to sell it.

I nodded as I listened to her talk. She'd been kind enough to allow me to provide the gelato for the inn's guests when she heard I'd been struggling during our last Red Stiletto Book Club meeting.

I wanted to hide it. I didn't want people to know how bad things had gotten, but it had tumbled out, and before I could hurriedly backtrack, everyone in the group had their attention on me. At that point, there was no use hiding it, so I told them everything.

Every last embarrassing, soul-crushing detail.

One of the great things about living in a small town, people rally around you to help if they sense your struggle. Soon I was getting orders from the inn, from the diner, and orders for personal drop-offs to people's homes. I doubled my sales in just a few short weeks, which was nice, but I doubted the longevity of it.

Which was why winning the annual fishing competition was so important to me. I could get out from under the stress of my finances for a few months and come up with a game plan for what my future would look like.

I didn't like being backed into a corner where I was expected to decide what was going to happen to me with only irrational emotions as my guide. I wanted to be wise and make decisions based on logic. Having the funds from the fishing competition would help me decide the best route for me to take, because I would have time to think about it.

"This competition has been a godsend for us," Maggie said as she stretched her arms out and curved her back. She smiled over at me, and I just nodded. "It seems everyone is renting a room at the inn so they can participate."

I pushed on my blinker and turned into the inn's parking lot. I found the only empty space and pulled in.

"Wanna come in for a quick coffee?" she asked.

I thought about agreeing but then shook my head. "I've gotta go get ready. Tonight marks the start of the weekend madness. I need to be there at five p.m. sharp."

Maggie chuckled as she pulled open the passenger door. "Well, good luck. I'm sure you're going to kill it." She hopped onto the ground and then turned to smile at me. "If you need anything, just call."

I gave her a quick salute and then waited as she pulled the bags of sheets from the bed of the truck and hurried across the parking lot and up the front stairs of the inn. I pulled out of the lot and watched as Archer opened the door and took the bags from Maggie. He gave me a quick wave, and I returned the gesture as I drove past. And just before I cleared the parking lot, I saw someone who I thought had moved on from Magnolia.

My entire body halted, and somehow, my foot found the brake. I came to a screeching halt loud enough to make the one person I didn't want to see turn around and stare straight at me.

Benjamin Williams.

I was right. He was there, standing in front of me. All

his six-foot-something of annoying handsomeness. He'd cut his hair from its previous shaggy length, complete with a beard. It still had some length as it fell across his forehead in an annoying way that made me want to brush it off. His eyebrows rose as I felt his gaze sweep over me. Then he smiled. In his annoying, cocky way.

My skin heated as I gathered my wits and gripped the steering wheel until I was pretty sure it would yelp in protest.

In Magnolia, the Browns did not get along with the Williams. Not when the Williams clan blew into town and opened a rival ice cream chain. My grandmother was forced to shut down all but one of her gelato stores because of their undercutting her prices. They had since sold their company and moved out of town, but not before their work did its intended damage.

Damage to me and my family.

I glowered at him as I drove past, making sure there was no questioning my feelings toward him. Ben studied me before turning to focus on Levi, his best friend and lackey while he'd lived here. Levi was talking, and whatever he said must have been funny because, just as I pulled out of view, I saw Ben let out his signature full-hearted laugh.

It rang in my ears as I drove all the way back to the small gelato shack off of Magnolia Beach. I felt agitated as I grabbed the bags of ingredients and hopped out of the truck. Heat pricked at my neck as I shoved all the items into spots where they would fit and then sat down on the barstool that sat against the far wall and took in a deep breath.

So many questions were running through my mind as I stared off into the distance.

What was Ben Williams doing back in Magnolia?

Was he here for good?

And was I going to have to interact with him?

I scrubbed my face with my hands as I tried to calm my emotions down. Whatever he was here for, it wasn't for me. So I needed to try my best to not let it bother me. My goal for the weekend was to win the competition so I could figure out where things were going from here.

It wasn't my goal to get caught up in my emotions over seeing someone who I thought had moved on and who I'd rather forget. I stood and headed toward the small one-bedroom apartment behind the gelato shop. I hurried to shove a few pieces of clothing into my backpack along with my toothbrush, hairbrush, and deodorant.

It wasn't required that you stay the night at the pier, but I was determined to win. The biggest catch was mine to reel in. I wanted to be there as long as I possibly could to make that dream a reality.

I glanced down at my watch and saw that I had thirty minutes to get to the Magnolia pier. After throwing up the *closed for the weekend* sign, I grabbed my phone charger and beach chair and threw them into the bed of my truck. I climbed into the cab, and my wheels spun as I peeled out of the lot and onto the main road.

When I came to a stop sign, I hurriedly gathered my

curly red hair up into a messy bun at the top of my head and returned my hands to the wheel. I pressed on the gas and made it to the pier's parking lot with minutes to spare.

I pulled the keys from the ignition and opened my door. I jumped down, shoved my keys into my back pocket and made my way to the back to grab my stuff.

I could hear the mayor testing the microphone, and I peeked over my shoulder to see that a crowd had already gathered in front of the small stage that bands played on during weekend farmers markets or evening parties. I slung my backpack over my shoulder followed by my beach chair, which was in a small bag with a strap.

I grabbed my water bottle and took a giant sip. Just as my mouth filled with water, a very familiar voice sounded from behind me. It startled me, and before I could stop myself, before my brain could register what Ben had just said to me, I tipped my head up and spit the water that had been inside my mouth all over him.

All over him.

2

I wanted to feel bad, I did. After all, Ben looked as if he'd just been waterboarded. Beads of water rolled down his face and dripped off his chin and nose—but I didn't feel bad. Not in the slightest.

I wiped at my lips at the same time Ben reached up and squeegeed his face. He then wiped his face with the hem of his shirt, all the while exposing his six-pack that, of course, he had.

I dragged my gaze up to meet his because there was no way I was going to be caught staring at Benjamin Williams' stomach, no matter how rock-hard his abs looked.

Blast him.

"Well, you certainly know how to make an old friend feel welcomed," he said as his ridiculous half-smile that had weakened the knees of most of the women in Magnolia crept across his lips.

He may be able to fool the other residents in town but not me. I knew how scummy he was. I knew that all his good looks and charms were there to hide the snake underneath.

"You feel welcomed? Well, then I'm not doing my job," I said as I sidestepped him and began to make my way toward the small card table that had been set up for registration. Patsy was sitting behind the table, smiling up at what looked like an out-of-towner who was finishing up paying.

"Scar."

I felt Ben's hand on my elbow, and I yanked it away before he could get a hold on me. There was no way I was going to just stand there and pretend to exchange pleasantries with Ben. His family had picked a side and so had I. We weren't anything to each other. The only thing he owed me was an apology, which, from the conversation we had before he left three months ago, wasn't going to happen. So the fact that he was following me just made me feel…annoyed.

"Hey, Scar, honey. Signing up for the competition?" Patsy asked as she shielded her eyes with one hand and handed the clipboard to me with the other. I gave her a smile as I took it from her.

I stepped to the side so I could fill out the form without blocking others from approaching. After it was filled out, I got back in line. Just as I moved forward a spot, I glanced behind me to see that Ben was standing there with a clipboard in hand. I furrowed my brow as I stared at it.

"No," I said as I shook my head. "You're not competing, are you?" I asked as I pointed my finger at his filled-out form.

He furrowed his brow as he studied me. "And what if I was?"

"You don't live here. You left. Why…" I tried to form my thoughts around what was happening, but nothing was working. My brain felt as if it had halted mid-thought.

Ben sighed as he tucked the clipboard under his arm and raised his hand in front of my face, snapping his fingers a few times. "You okay?" he asked.

I blinked as reality came crashing down around me. Ben Williams was back in my life. He was back in my town, and I had no idea what his angle was or what he was planning on doing, but it couldn't be good.

I swallowed and spun back around. My heart was racing as I tried to figure out what I was going to do. The only thing that came to mind was my grandmother's voice, telling me to take a deep breath. *Things always look different when you have more oxygen in your body*, she would tell me.

After taking in as much air as my lungs were capable of holding, I began to feel a tad dizzy. The last thing I needed was to faint in front of Ben. So I stilled my mind as I approached Patsy and handed her the clipboard with the twenty-dollar entrance fee.

I could do this. I didn't have to talk to Ben. Sure, he was here for the competition, but so were a lot of people. It was a big beach. It wasn't like he was going to camp out next to me. If I tried hard enough, I wouldn't even have to see him.

And that thought gave me the confidence to walk over to the stage where Victoria Hold had started her obligatory welcome-to-the-competition speech. I stood around, half listening, half staring out at the water as she finished up. A cheer sounded and everyone began to move to the pier or spots on the beach that they'd reserved.

I pulled my backpack higher up onto my shoulder as I hurried to the pier to find the spot I'd marked off for myself. It was the prime location. My grandfather brought me here to fish so many times, I'd lost count. He would set up our chairs three feet from the pier's edge and he would tell me the story of how he caught a forty-pound bluefish.

It was his own personal Moby Dick.

I would laugh and listen while we ate sunflower seeds and the leftover gelato granny would bring us after the shop closed. His story got more outlandish every time he told it.

I'd fall asleep and find myself magically transported to my bed the next morning. Then I'd beg mom to let me go back out. This time we'd find grandpa's bluefish and he would be vindicated, even if all the townspeople doubted his story.

So for this competition, it was a no-brainer that this was the location I would fish from. I patted the small tent

I'd set up earlier that day and slipped my chair off my shoulder and out of its bag. I shook out the chair and set it next to the cooler that I'd stocked with all sorts of goodies. After tossing my backpack into the tent, I focused on my fishing pole.

By this time, it was better to use a tube and worm rig or live bait, and since I didn't want to have to continually restock my bait fish, I went with the former. After all, if I could catch a striped bass, my chances of winning were even greater.

Just as I finished prepping my pole, movement next to me drew my attention over. It took a few seconds, but when Ben's face clearly came into view, I couldn't help but groan.

"Well, this is interesting," he said as he dumped his backpack into a taped-off square and stretched his arms above his head.

It seemed as if he were purposely avoiding my gaze as he kept his focus out on the ocean. The sun was inches above the horizon, and its final rays were casting a range of oranges and purples across the sky. On any other night, I would have said it looked beautiful. But the thought of Ben sitting next to me this entire competition left a sour taste in my mouth.

He was going to ruin my weekend and my chances of winning.

"Can't you go somewhere else?" I asked as I prepped my pole and then cast the line into the water. The rig dropped under the surface, and I set the end of my pole in a dug out spot on the pier that my grandfather *may* have been responsible for.

Ben scoffed.

I glowered over at him. What kind of response was that?

Ben must have felt my icy gaze because, a moment later, he glanced up at me and shrugged. "You don't own the pier, Scarlett. Others can fish here as well. It just so happens that we both know the best spot." He shrugged. "Forgive me for wanting to have the best chance at winning."

"Oh, you won't be winning." I tightened my ponytail and stared with determination out to where I'd dropped my line. He had to be joking if he thought that he was going to win. I was a Brown. Fishing was in our blood.

"Ooo, that sounds like a challenge."

I peeked over at Ben to see him smiling at me. I'm not a normally angry person. If anything, I had an uncanny ability to find the good in every situation. But apparently, that gift didn't apply to a Williams. Try as I might—and I might not be trying that hard—there was nothing good I could find when it came to Ben.

"Not so much a challenge as it is a fact," I said as I opened up my cooler and pulled out my bag of sunflower seeds.

"Care to make a wager, then?"

I turned my attention to him. "A bet?"

He nodded. "Sure. Bet. Wager. Friendly competition."

I narrowed my eyes at him. "What would I win?"

He scoffed as he moved around, prepping his own fishing pole. "Wow. You're that confident."

"I've lived in Magnolia my whole life. I've fished these waters since I was a kid." I turned my attention back out to the ocean. "I didn't just move in, crush a family in the process, and leave," I muttered under my breath. If Ben heard me, he didn't acknowledge it.

He was too busy focusing on casting his line and then settling down in his chair. I popped a few sunflower seeds while I chewed on his proposal. What would it hurt if I entered into a little competition with Ben? After all, it might help pass the time. And if it ended with me taking something from a Williams, all the better.

"Alright. I'm on board," I said as I turned to face him.

He raised his eyebrows. "Really?"

I nodded. "Yep. Let's do this. Just know I'm going to crush you." I didn't soften my stance as I studied him. He had to know what he was getting into by proposing this to me.

"I'll consider myself warned."

I pursed my lips and gave him a resolute nod. "So, what are we wagering?"

He scrubbed his face. "Let's start small and work our way up."

I eyed him. "Okay."

He shrugged. "First person to get a catch wins."

"Wins what?"

He glanced down, and then when he shifted his gaze back up to me, I wasn't sure how I felt about the smile that appeared. It wasn't forced. It wasn't mocking. It felt…genuine.

And I wasn't sure how to interpret it.

I knew I should have backed out at that moment, but something inside of me didn't want to. Instead, I wanted to know just what his angle was. What exactly he was going to try to get out of me. So I let him continue.

"I think the perfect reward should be dinner. Provided by the loser."

3

He had to be joking.

That was the only way to read his suggestion.

Dinner? With him? Why?

I snorted and shook my head.

"You think that's a reward? That sounds like torture to me." I picked up my fishing pole and jerked it a few times. Then I returned it back to its holder and peeked back at Ben, who was still watching me.

He must have noticed my gaze because, a moment later, he turned his focus back to the ocean. "It's just a meal, Scarlett. And I don't know about you, but I'm feeling like I'll be ready to eat in a few hours." He tapped his watch.

As if on cue, my stomach growled. Sure, I had snacks in my cooler, but that was only going to last for so long. If

I was going to outlast my competition and win the prize, I was going to need sustenance.

And the idea of Ben Williams paying for my meal was too good to pass up. So I sighed and nodded. "Fine. I was really wanting a porterhouse steak tonight." Galileo, one of the fancy restaurants on the island, was known for their steaks.

"Porterhouse steak?" Ben asked.

"Yep. For when I win and you have to pay." I grinned over at him.

Ben studied me and then his smile returned. That annoying smile that I couldn't quite figure out. No one could be that nice, that relaxed with a history like ours. He definitely had an angle, and it was my job to figure it out.

We were rivals. He had to know that, and yet, the way he was smiling at me—looking at me—told me that he didn't understand that. And it was frustrating me.

"So do we have a deal?" Ben asked as he crossed the small space between us and extended his hand.

I studied it for a moment and then nodded. "Yep. I guess," I said as I slipped my hand in his, and for a moment—one inexplicable moment—a small current of electricity rushed up my arm. I quickly retracted my hand and pushed away any thoughts of what a reaction like that would mean.

I couldn't think of Ben as anything more than my rival. Plain and simple. And confusing myself would only distract me from my goal right now. Which was winning this competition.

I focused my attention on the ocean and settled back in my seat. I felt calmer, which was strange. Especially since the person I'd decided to hate forever was seated next to me. I doubted that there was even five feet between us. So the fact that I could actually take in deep breaths and not feel like the world was collapsing around me was a feat in and of itself.

"Lots of changes since I was last here." Ben's voice drifted over to me. I turned to see him glancing at me. So I had been right. He was talking to me.

I nodded and decided to reel in my line and cast again. I wasn't sure what I was supposed to say to that. Was he asking me a question or just trying to make small talk?

I honestly didn't want to participate in it either way. I was here to fish and relax. Not to fix a relationship that was never going to be fixed.

Once my line was cast, I settled back in my seat and pulled our current book club read from my backpack. We were reading *Little Women*. A book I read as a kid, and yet, as an adult, my appreciation for it had only grown.

Minutes ticked by, and yet, my book wasn't holding my attention like I'd hoped it would. I found myself peeking over at Ben, who was busy scrolling through things on his phone. I darted my gaze back to my book when I saw him turn his head to glance over at me.

Heat permeated my cheeks as I stared at the words on the page. I wasn't reading anything, but Ben didn't know that.

"Is it a good book?" Ben asked.

I nodded and turned the page—not having read anything on it but desperate to appear as if I had.

"You seem to be enjoying it."

"Yes," I said. Then I sighed, stuck my finger in-between the pages as a place holder, and turned to face him. "We have a book club meeting next week and I need to have it read before then."

"Book club?"

I grabbed my actual bookmark from my lap and slipped it inside. Then I tucked the book back into my backpack. "Maggie and Clementine started it up. Apparently, it started years ago at the inn and they decided to revive it." I shrugged. "It's fun."

Ben nodded along with my words. He seemed like he was really listening, which was strange. Why was he taking such an interest in me? It was unnerving.

The desire to keep talking washed over me, so I parted my lips and spoke. Maybe I was afraid that if I stopped, he'd speak. And not knowing what he wanted to talk about made me feel uneasy.

"We've only been doing it for a few months. But it's nice. We've become closer friends, and it's helped Maggie. You know, it can be hard to move into a small town. Where everyone already knows everyone. Fitting in can be hard." I pinched my lips together to get myself to stop talking. Why did I feel the need to blab on and on? Ben didn't ask for the book club's story and yet, here I was, giving it.

When I glanced over at him, I noticed that he was not

only smiling, but his head was also tipped toward me. As if he had actually listened to my word vomit.

I blinked a few times and then shook my head. I had to be imagining things. If he was listening, it was out of obligation, not out of interest. He'd asked a simple question, and I'd spiraled out of control. I was the one who was reading into things, not Ben.

And if I didn't watch myself, I'd make a much bigger mistake than I could handle. I couldn't actually start to *like* Ben as a human being. He was my rival. My enemy. There was no way we could be anything more than that. I was pretty sure my mind and heart didn't know how to handle that.

Needing something to do, I reeled in my line and grabbed the fishing line to steady my lure. I took in a deep breath as I attempted to get control of my head and my thoughts. I didn't need to make a verbal mistake and not be able to take it back. I needed all my wits about me if I was going to attempt to continue our conversation.

"Listen to me," I said as I shook my head, "blathering on like you actually wanted to listen to any of that." I played with the fishing line as I strained to hear what Ben was going to say in response.

I heard him chuckle, which I took as a good sign. At least he wasn't annoyed. If he was annoyed, then he would probably try to figure out what was wrong with me. If he was trying to tie those lines together, then he would most likely land on the thought that, perhaps, I was nervous.

And if he thought I was nervous, then he would start to assume all sorts of ungodly things.

Things that he could never think about me.

Like that he made my brain short-circuit when he was around.

"I don't mind it."

His words startled me, and my hand jerked, sending searing hot pain shooting through my finger, up my arm, and exploding in my brain. I yelped and pulled my hand back from the pole only to see that I'd successfully shoved the hook into my finger.

"Ouch," I cried out before I could stop myself.

Suddenly, Ben was next to me. He cradled my hand in his, and the only thing I could think about was how small my hands looked next to his. And then pain brought me screaming back to reality.

"Are you okay?" he asked.

I pinched my lips together as tears sprang up in my eyes. I didn't want to cry—I didn't want to show weakness in front of Ben—but it was a physical reaction to pain, and no matter how much I tried to stop them, the tears flowed.

Ben turned and guided me over to his chair. He pressed his hand on my shoulder and I obediently sat. Blood and I didn't mix, and from the pool gathering in his hand, it was a gusher.

He busied himself with grabbing his first aid kit, because, of course, I'd forgotten mine. Then he knelt in front of me as he began removing the hook. I winced and yelped as it slid from my skin. Ben already had gauze in his hand and instantly wrapped it around my finger. He glanced up at me and offered me an apologetic smile.

"Sorry," he said.

I wanted to say something, but I couldn't find it in my brain to speak. He was close—too close. When he was this near, I could see the gold flecks in his green eyes and the splash of freckles across his nose. I could smell his cologne as I stared at his hair that was annoyingly draped across his forehead again.

When I was this close to him, I could see him as a human. And not only as a human, I could see him as a… man. And those thoughts were causing my mind to fog and my stomach to lighten.

I was feeling things that I hadn't felt in a long time, and I was pretty sure he was the last guy I wanted to feel them for.

He was Ben Williams. Off limits. I wasn't supposed to see him as anything but my enemy.

Duh.

Thankfully, he kept his attention on my finger as he cleaned my wound and bandaged it up. When he released me and focused on putting back all the items he'd taken out, I pulled my hand back and grasped it with my other hand. For some reason, I could still feel his hand on mine.

It was like his touch was burned on my skin, and even though my finger was throbbing, that was the feeling that was dominating my thoughts right now.

I cleared my throat and stood. "Thanks," I said.

Ben clicked his med kit closed and then stood up as well. Apparently, I'd misjudged the distance between us, and suddenly, he was staring down at me from only inches away. Like, my lips were inches below his. If he wanted to, he could lean down and brush his lips to mine.

Idiot.

What was wrong with me? It must be the lack of blood flowing through my body. Or the sudden rush that I got from standing up too fast.

Yes. That had to be it.

There couldn't be any other reason for why I would be thinking about Ben's lips or the fact that I was really interested in what it might feel like to have his arms wrapped around me…

I needed to get out of here. I needed to get to my side of the pier, where I was safe. Where there was some distance between us.

Thankfully, I had enough sense to take a few steps back just as Ben nodded and shoved his hands into his front pockets.

"Yeah, sure. Anytime." His smile flashed on his lips, and suddenly, I couldn't think straight.

Before I allowed myself to say something I might regret, I gave him a quick nod and got the heck out of there. When I got back to my chair, I collapsed on it and blew out my breath.

Well, that had been completely unexpected.

4

The air between us had changed. And I wasn't sure if it was because of me or because of him. Or because we had just stood within inches of each other and the idea of kissing him—*kissing* Benjamin Williams—had actually entered my mind.

I shook my head as I cast my line and set my pole back into its holder. The throbbing in my finger had died down to a manageable ache, so I decided that moving forward with the competition was the best possible option. The fish weren't going to catch themselves.

Plus, when I was busy, there was no reason for me to cross the line into his space, and there was equally no reason for him to cross the line into mine. We could both lose ourselves in the competition and never speak to each other again.

If we kept to our individual areas, there would be no opportunity for ridiculous thoughts to enter my mind.

And my momentary lack of judgement would only be a blip on my radar. A mistake in my past that I would never have to think of again.

If I thought that way, then I was sure I could survive. I was sure I'd be fine.

Thankfully, Ben didn't seem to want to talk either, and it felt as if an hour had passed before he spoke again.

"Feeling better?"

I blinked and straightened in my chair. For a moment there, I'd almost nodded off. "Hmm?" I asked as I turned to see him standing with his hands shoved into his front pockets on the tape that separated our spaces. He was squinting at me. The sun had almost completely disappeared behind the horizon and the stars were beginning to sparkle above us.

"Your finger. How does it feel?"

I glanced down and flexed my fingers a few times. As I did, pained jolted through my hand. I winced but forced a smile. "It's better."

He furrowed his brow. "You might want to get that checked out. It was pretty deep, and who knows what kind of bacteria got in there."

I shook my head. "I'll survive. It's not my first time spearing myself, and I'm pretty sure it won't be my last." I stretched my arms and legs out in front of me. I shivered and looked around for my blanket. My stomach growled, and I realized that neither of us had caught anything all evening. If one of us didn't catch something soon, I was going to starve.

"Still, it might be a good idea, just in case."

I narrowed my eyes in his direction. "Are you just wanting to get me out of the competition?"

Ben snorted and turned to face the ocean. "Not everything is about competition. Sometimes life matters more than winning." H spoke under his breath as if he didn't intend for me to hear it.

Frustration boiled up inside of me at his words. Maybe for him winning didn't matter, but for me, it mattered a whole lot. I wasn't going to let a little poke to my finger stop me from reaching my goal.

I let out a huff and turned back to my line just in time to see the pole of Ben's fishing rod bend. The sound of the reel engaging rang in my ears. I'd recognize that sound anywhere.

He'd hooked a fish.

He rushed over to his pole and lifted it out of the holder. He began to wind and tug as he reeled the fish in. Whatever it was, it was big.

I couldn't help but watch him. As a player of the game, the same adrenaline that I was sure was pumping through his veins was pumping through mine. It was that feeling you get when you catch a fish.

Even though Ben was my rival. Even though I knew I should be upset that he was one fish ahead of me in the chance to win this competition, I did feel a tad relieved. He had won our first bet, which meant food was in my future even if our score tally was now tipping in Ben's favor.

Ben: 1

Scarlett: 0

Despite that thought rolling around in my mind, I couldn't help but sit riveted in my seat as I watched him reel in the fish.

Inside I was cheering for him. I didn't want his line to break. I didn't want the fish to slip away. All I wanted was to see the mammoth on the line that was giving him a heck of a struggle.

It took a good ten minutes of fighting until Ben got the fish close enough so that he could slip his net into the water and scoop it up. A cheer sounded across the pier as he held up what looked like a good fifteen-pound bluefish. It was big, but it wasn't competition-winning big.

A sigh of relief slipped from my lips as I collapsed back onto my chair. The adrenaline in the air was palpable, and it was taking a moment for my own heart rate to slow to its normal pace.

From the corner of my eye, I saw Ben remove his hook and then, a moment later, slip the fish back into the water. Confused, I glanced over at him.

"You're not keeping it?"

He shook his head as he prepped his hook and cast his line back into the water. "Nah. I'm going back home after the competition. I don't really want to bring a bunch of fish back with me."

I kept my gaze trained on the water as I chewed on his words. I'd never learned where he'd moved to or what he was doing. And despite my better judgement, I kind of wanted to know. What had caused him to move off island? Was he ruining another gelato owner's livelihood like he'd done with me?

I winced at my own thoughts. As much as I wanted to believe that Ben was no good and his only reason for living was to make other people miserable, I knew it wasn't true. It was easier to hate someone when they weren't around. It's hard to believe those thoughts when the person is staring straight at you.

Which was what he was doing right now.

I blinked a few times to bring myself back to reality. It wouldn't look good for me to zone out while looking in his direction. The last thing I needed was for him to assume that my momentary lapse in judgement meant anything.

Because it didn't.

It really didn't.

Once the commotion settled down and Ben was sitting in his chair, I let out my breath in an attempt to compose myself. Then, I turned to look at him.

"So what do you want for dinner?"

He glanced over at me and then reached down to grab his water bottle and took a sip. "It's okay," he said quietly.

I shook my head. I was a woman of my word. If I agreed to a bet, I was going to follow through. "Nope. We agreed. And if I had won, I would have made you do it." I clicked my imaginary pen and raised the palm of my other hand as a notepad. "What do you require?"

He furrowed his brow as he turned to look at me. I

raised my eyebrows and gave him an expectant look. There was no way I was going to let him turn me down.

I shrugged as I continued to hold up my hands. "If you don't tell me, I'm just going to order what I want, and you'll have to eat it."

He studied me for a moment longer before he chuckled and settled back in his chair. "I could go for the fatty burger and chocolate malt from Shakes."

At those words, my stomach growled. Sure, it was an artery-clogging hamburger with layers of cheese and bacon nestled inside a homemade hamburger bun, but it was delicious. Ben certainly knew how to pick 'em.

I nodded as I grabbed my phone and typed his order.

Burger with no onions and extra pickles and a chocolate shake.

"No fries?" I asked as my thumbs hovered over the keyboard, waiting for his response.

"Sure, a serving of fries."

I nodded. "Great. I'll text Mags to pick it up. She said she'd help me out if I needed it." I stood and brought my phone to my ear.

"You're not going to go get it?" he asked as he straightened.

I stared down at him. "I've got a competition to win. I'm not wasting a minute."

Ben nodded as he turned back toward the ocean. I spent the next five minutes calling Brenda at Shakes to place the order and then texting Maggie. She was so sweet and even said that she and Archer had placed an order as well, so the timing worked out perfectly.

I tucked my phone into my back pocket and returned to my chair, where I fiddled with my line just to make sure everything was working. I reeled in my line, adjusted a few things, and cast it back out into the ocean.

"Maggie's on her way to pick up dinner," I said.

Ben glanced over at me and nodded. "Perfect. I'm getting hungry."

We fished in silence until the sound of someone walking on the pier caused me to turn around. Maggie was walking toward us with a plastic bag in hand. When she met my gaze, she smiled and waved.

I stood and walked over to her. She gave me a quick hug and then handed the bag of food over.

"I'm sorry I'm so late. You know Brenda. She was chatty tonight. Shakes was in full swing, and I think the adrenaline was getting to her." Maggie's cheeks were pink as she smiled over at me.

I nodded. "You're a lifesaver. We're starving."

Maggie furrowed her brow as she glanced behind me. "We?"

Embarrassment crept up inside of me as I pinched my lips together. Had I just classified Ben and I as *we*? When had that happened?

I cleared my throat and laughed off my blunder. "Just Ben Williams and I. We had a little friendly bet going, and I lost." I hugged the food containers to my chest as I peeked up to see Maggie studying me.

"Ben Williams."

I shivered as Ben's voice sounded behind me. He was only inches away. Suddenly, his hand appeared. He was so close to me that I could feel his warmth against my back even though he wasn't touching me.

All my senses were on high alert as I contemplated throwing the food at him and taking off down the pier. Something between us was changing. And I wasn't sure I was okay with it happening. I wasn't supposed to have feelings toward Ben. Especially not feelings that had my stomach in knots and my palms sweating.

This was wrong. It was all wrong.

"It's nice to meet you," Maggie said as they shook hands for a few seconds. "I'm Maggie. I own Magnolia Inn."

Ben chuckled and his hand disappeared. I could only assume that he dropped it to his side. "I heard last time I was here. You stirred up quite a commotion."

Maggie smiled. "It's been good. The inn filled a hole I didn't know existed." Her eyes grew misty and a soft smile spread across her lips. She fanned her face and blew out her breath. "Listen to me. Getting all sappy."

She turned her attention to me. "I've got to get going. If I don't get back, Archer's going to be upset."

I nodded and she handed the tray of shakes over to me.

"Good luck. Call me if you need anything more."

I held the shakes as I thanked her and then watched her turn and head back down the pier. It took a few seconds for me to compose myself as I took in a deep breath. Strange things were happening to me, and I wasn't sure that I liked any of it. I wasn't here to develop strange feelings for Ben. I was here for one purpose and one purpose only.

To win.

Somehow, I'd allowed myself to forget that. Or at least, to get distracted by Ben's smile and his ridiculous dimple. I'd allowed myself to forget that he was my enemy—everything he said seemed to point to a different conclusion. He wasn't a fire-breathing monster whose family had blown into town and wrecked mine.

For some reason, I was allowing myself to believe that, perhaps, he was a nice person. And, perhaps, I could like said person.

Which was wrong. It was so wrong.

Ben Williams was the same as always, no matter what my heart was trying to tell me. At some point, he was going to stab me in the back. It was just the way of things with a Williams. And if I wasn't careful, I was going to end this competition with an injured heart.

And I couldn't have that.

I wasn't sure that I would survive.

5

Thankfully, we had food to distract us, and as soon as I settled into my seat with my burger on my lap and my shake on the pier next to me, all my thoughts of Ben and my worries associated with him went flying out the window. All I could think about was the warmth of the burger as I bit into it and the explosion of flavor as I chewed.

And Ben seemed to be equally distracted.

When my food was gone and I felt as if I was going to explode, I settled back into my chair and rested my hands on my stomach. There was such a feeling of satisfaction that came from eating a good meal that, all of a sudden, my previous freak-outs didn't seem to matter anymore. At least, not to the extent that they had when I was bite-your-head-off starving.

Right now, through the cloudy haze of a fatty burger, I was beginning to realize that it was a tad ridiculous to think that I had feelings for Ben. Or at least, that I was starting to think of him as someone other than my enemy. He was just a person I had a past with. That was all. There was no need for me to read into things and, in the process, get confused.

It was just hard, being this physically close to him. When he wasn't around, I could convince myself that I didn't care. That I was never going to care. But when he was right next to me, it was hard for me ignore him.

I took in a deep breath. I had to ignore him. By the end of the competition, he would be gone, and I would go back to normal life and this whole experience would be just a moment in my past. One that I was sure I could forget.

I would forget.

"Can I take your trash?"

Ben's voice startled me, and I jolted upright to see him standing next to me. He held out the bag that Maggie had brought the food in.

I cleared my throat and gathered up my garbage. "Thanks," I murmured as I dumped it into the bag.

Ben nodded and then disappeared down the pier. I blew out my breath as I turned my attention back to the ocean. What was wrong with me? Why did I turn into a bumbling idiot every time he was around?

He had to notice that something was off. He had to be suspicious that I was creating a mess inside of myself over my own ridiculous thoughts. He had to feel the change in my demeanor when he came around.

Apparently, being a spy was not in my future because there was no way I could be stealthy. I was as obvious as a blowhorn.

Just call me Blowhorn Scarlett.

I sighed as I tucked my blanket around my shoulders and buried my face into the soft folds of the fabric. Movement next to me drew my attention over. Ben was walking down the pier. He looked distracted, and for a moment, I allowed my gaze to drift over him.

He was tall and broad. Time had definitely allowed him to fill out more. His hair shifted in the breeze, and the moon above shone down on him, illuminating his blond hair in its light. I found my breath catching in my throat as I studied him.

Had he always been this handsome? Or did I hit my head and not know it. Like in those movies where they suddenly start seeing people differently?

Was I seeing Ben differently? What did that mean?

Fear crept up inside of me, and the only rational thing I could think of was to drop my gaze and pinch my eyes closed. Maybe, if I tried hard enough, I could wish this situation away. This situation where my feelings were growing for the last person I should have feelings for.

The smell of the salt air and the sound of the waves below me helped calm my ragged nerves. I took in a few deep breaths and allowed my body to sink into the fabric of my chair. The darkness of the world outside helped me to relax. Here, I was safe. Here, inside of my mind, Ben didn't exist.

"Want a s'more?"

Until he spoke.

And then, he existed everywhere.

I peeked over to see him standing there with a bag of marshmallows in one hand and a package of chocolate bars in the other. Confused, I opened both eyes and turned to focus on him.

"How? There's no place for a fire."

Ben smiled and tucked the chocolate bars under his arm so he could hold up his finger. "Oh, ye of little faith," he said as he dumped the stuff onto his chair and, suddenly, passed over the protective line of tape to set his chair next to mine. Then he adjusted the s'more stuff so he could sit down.

I eyed him as he set down the marshmallows, chocolate, and graham crackers onto the pier and lifted up something I couldn't quite make out in the darkness. Then there was a clicking sound and a flash of light. Ben was smiling ridiculously wide behind a single flame as he studied me.

"A lighter? That's how we are going to toast our marshmallows?"

He nodded as he produced a fork and speared a marshmallow with it. "S'mores are a staple when you fish," he said as he held the marshmallow next to the flame.

"Staple?"

He nodded. "My dad used to take me fishing every weekend."

My stomach squeezed at the mention of his family, but

after one look at his downturned expression, I felt confused. He looked sad, and that stirred something inside me. Instead of indifference, I found myself wanting to know why he looked that way. What had happened?

"Used to?" I asked slowly. Did I really want to know? Knowing would deepen our relationship, and I wasn't sure I wanted to do that. Did I want to have that kind of relationship with Ben? If I started down this path, there was no going back.

Ben cleared his throat and glanced out to the ocean before he looked at me. "Dad passed away last year. Cancer." His voice was so quiet that I feared the wind would pick it up and whisk it away before I heard him. I leaned in, and as soon as those words met my ears, my heart ached.

I knew what that loss was like. My grandpa had passed away from prostate cancer. It was the hardest and worst moment of my life. "I'm so sorry," I said as tears sprung up in my eyes.

Ben was looking at me when I turned my attention to him. His eyes looked as tearful as mine. "Thanks," he said softly. "It was hard. Mom has kind of closed in on herself. She's not the same." He blew out his breath as he turned the fork so he could toast another side of the marshmallow. "I'm not the same. He left me a company that I don't really want to run."

And there it was. Everything that I didn't want to hear in one short little sentence.

It felt as if he'd stabbed my stomach with a bunch of

knives. *A company he doesn't really want to run.* The company that had ruined my family. The one that was the reason I would have to close the doors on my grandmother's life work. And yet, he didn't want it.

It was a nuisance for him.

I sucked in the night air as if I hoped it would help cool my agitated emotions. I knew that wasn't what he was saying. He wasn't trying to stomp on the memory of my family—even though it felt that way. But I couldn't help but feel upset. Upset with my situation and upset with the fact that Ben didn't seem to notice.

But it shouldn't matter if Ben didn't understand—that was what I was trying to tell myself. This was a weekend acquaintanceship. That was all. We weren't friends. That wasn't in the cards for us.

We were just two people sitting next to each other in a fishing competition. Our conversations were there only to fill the silence as we waited. That was all.

We were never meant to go deeper than surface level in our relationship.

I knew that, and yet, I was having a hard time implementing it in my mind.

Taking in a deep breath, I decided to focus on my pole. I'd had a few nibbles about ten minutes ago, and I was waiting to see if I was going to get a bite. I needed the win. I needed some sort of action to take place on my pole. Not only to further my chances of winning this competition, but also for the distraction it was going to give me. The distraction from Ben and how confused I felt when we spoke.

If Ben noticed my withdrawal, he didn't comment on it. Instead, he continued twisting the marshmallow over the flame and talking. He talked about his new job as a landscaper—his change in build now made sense. He talked about his dog and how he'd found the perfect lake to fish on in Pennsylvania—apparently, that was where he'd settled down.

I nodded as I listened, but I kept my gaze focused on the dark ocean water. The moon shone against it, giving an eerie, yet calming ambiance. It seemed to be what I needed to calm my nerves.

Just as Ben finished building a s'more and moved to hand it over to me, my fishing reel engaged, and suddenly, my pole was bending. My heart picked up speed as I leapt off my chair and hurried to grab the pole and reel. Any confusing thoughts I had before this flew from my mind, and all I could focus on was reeling in this fish.

In the moment, I could see all my issues with the gelato shop fly out the window. This was going to be my saving grace. This was going to give me the win for the competition, and I was finally going to get that much-needed break.

Ten minutes later, I was grinning from ear to ear as I dumped a twenty-pound bluefish into my net that I had hanging off the edge of the pier. He flipped around a few times, but as soon as I settled the net into the water, he calmed down.

I brought my wrist to my forehead and dabbed a few times. I'd broken a sweat reeling that bad boy in, and my body was still shivering from the adrenaline that was coursing through me because of the struggle. There had been a moment there where I thought I'd lost him, but Grandpa had taught me well. I knew how to sink a hook like a pro.

After wiping my hands, I turned to see that Ben was studying me with an amused expression on his face. He had set the s'more down on my seat and was busy toasting another marshmallow.

"Feel better?" he asked.

I nodded as I grabbed my s'more, taking a bite as I sat down in my chair. "Yeah, I needed that. I needed that win." The words were out before I could stop them.

Then they hung suspended in the air.

I peeked over at him to see if he'd picked up on it. Had he heard? Was he going to ask me what I meant? What was I going to tell him? There was no way I wanted to talk about how his family had ruined mine.

At least not right now.

Though, if I were honest with myself, I wasn't sure I wanted to *ever* have that conversation. Telling him how I felt meant that he would know more about me. He would see me as the raw, vulnerable person that I was. Especially when so much of my life lived in the land of the unknown. I hated that.

Why hadn't he come back when I had my crap

together? Why did he have to see me like this? At my lowest low.

"Everything okay?" he finally asked me. He kept his gaze focused on the marshmallow, and I could tell that he was hesitant. As if he was worried he'd overstepped.

And he had. Especially because he was the reason I was in this situation.

But I couldn't say those things. Not when I was beginning to realize that, perhaps, I had been wrong to assume that he was this big bad wolf who'd run into town and blown down all my family's hopes and dreams.

Someone who did that wouldn't take the time to talk to me.

Or cook me a s'more.

Or look at me like he was genuinely worried about me.

I blinked a few times as I allowed my gaze to linger on his. His brows were drawn together, and I could feel the concern in the depth of his eyes. He wanted to know.

Why did he want to know?

I started my response with a nod, and then slowly, I stopped moving. Tears sprung up in my eyes and I attempted to keep them at bay. I didn't want to cry. I was worried once I started, I wouldn't be able to stop.

Instead of delving deeper into my situation with Ben, I did the only thing I could think of. I downplayed the situation.

"I'm an adult. Is anything ever okay?" I forced a laugh as I shrugged and took a bite from my s'more.

I could feel Ben's focus on me, but thankfully, that only

lasted a moment before he sighed, nodded, and turned his focus back to his marshmallow.

Silence fell around us as we both focused on anything but the other person. Ben made a few more s'mores before he gathered his items and moved back over to his sectioned-off spot.

We spent the rest of the night fishing. I kept my focus on anything but Ben—but that was proving to be harder than I'd thought. I was tired and ready for a break.

So I closed my eyes, tipped my head back, and allowed my mind to go blank. If I fell asleep, good. At least in my dreams, I could pretend that I wasn't here.

That I wasn't confused by Ben.

In my dreams, my life could be perfect.

I could be happy.

And right now, that was all I wanted.

Happiness.

6

I stretched out in my tiny one-man tent and opened my eyes. The early morning light was barely up over the horizon, and its rays were shining through the tent fabric, illuminating it. I glanced around, confused how I'd even gotten in here.

The last thing I remembered was closing my eyes in my chair. Had I gotten up in the middle of the night and climbed into my tent?

That was a possibility, however from my experience, once I was out, I was out.

But with no other explanation as to why I was suddenly in my tent instead of my chair, that was the story I was going to go with.

I wiggled and stretched as I tried to increase the blood flow in my body. Sleeping on the hard pier probably wasn't the smartest move, but whatever. There was no way I was going to lose time in transit from my house back to the pier. If I wanted to win this competition, I needed all the time I could get.

I sat up in the tent and blew my breath into my hand. I winced at the smell. I felt the surfaces of my teeth and they felt disgusting. I needed a good brushing, that was for sure. I hastily combed my fingers through my hair and adjusted the sweatshirt that I was wearing. After grabbing my toothbrush and a change of clothes from my backpack, I hurried out of my tent, hoping to avoid Ben if at all possible.

Who knows what I did or said last night. If I could somehow stagger into my tent in the middle of the night without remembering it—what else did I do?

There was a small bathroom just off the pier, and since no one else was awake, or, if they were, they didn't seem to be paying attention to me, I hurried toward it. Thankfully, Ben's area was quiet. If I was lucky, I might be able to get some fishing done before he got up.

Once my teeth were brushed, my face rinsed, and my clothes changed, I felt like a new woman. I balled up my old clothes under my arm and pulled open the bathroom door only to walk straight into Ben.

His hands surrounded my arms as if he were trying to stop that from happening. As soon as I felt his grip, I froze. Like a deer in headlights.

I blinked a few times as I tried to ground myself. It was shocking to have him touch me. But even more shocking was the fact that he didn't let me go. Instead, he leaned in closer as if he were trying to catch my gaze.

"Are you okay?" he asked, his voice low. I wanted to believe he was being quiet because it was dawn and he hadn't spoken yet today, but the irrational and crazy part of me wanted to think that, perhaps, he was having the same reaction to our proximity as I was.

And then reality hit me, and thankfully, there was a part of my brain that was still able to get my body to move. I jumped back, breaking his grip on me. He was startled for a moment before he straightened and pushed his hands through his hair.

He looked apologetic, but I didn't want to hear him say sorry. I was pretty sure saying, *I didn't mean to touch you* was worse than the actual action. Sure, there was no way I wanted Ben to wrap his hands around my arms, hold me close, or stare at me like he had from only inches away. But I also didn't want him to take it back. I was sure that the blow to my self-esteem would be worse than his actual touch.

"I'm okay," I said hurriedly as I sidestepped him and half ran, half walked away from him.

If he said anything in response, I didn't hear it. Instead, I zeroed in on my spot on the pier and took off toward it. Once I got there, I shoved my dirty clothes into my backpack and began prepping my line to cast it into the ocean. According to the progress board, which I'd caught a quick look at as I headed toward the bathroom, the evening had been pretty quiet. Only a select few of us had actually caught anything that could put us in the running.

Bert, a lifelong resident and friend of my grandfather's,

was leading. I was number five on the list. If I wanted to have any chance, I needed to get moving.

The more I caught, the more chance I had of winning.

If I was going to accomplish this goal, I needed all the help I could get.

I let the fish I'd caught yesterday go. After all, if he wasn't going to clinch the victory for me, I might as well let him live a good life. After all, if he survived until next year, he just might be the winner for me then.

I waved at him as he slipped below the water's surface and away from the pier. I let out a sigh and focused on my pole. By the time I had my line cast, Ben was strolling up the pier. He looked more awake and refreshed with his hands shoved into his front pockets and his shoulders hunched upward. When he caught my gaze, he smiled.

I quickly turned my attention away from him and focused on the ocean. I figured it would be better to pretend that I didn't see him instead of trying to sort through how I was supposed to act around him. Things were definitely changing, I could feel it, no mistake about it.

But the part of me that was confused, the part that kept questioning everything about our situation, wasn't confused about how I felt.

It was about how *he* felt.

Or if he even felt anything.

I cleared my throat and blinked a few times as I forced my mind to clear. I was acting ridiculous right now. And when I acted this way, I made mistakes.

And I couldn't make a mistake. Not when it came to Ben.

"Sleep well?" he asked.

I peeked over at him to see that he was studying me with a smile twitching on his lips. I hated that butterflies erupted in my stomach when he looked at me. When he smiled at me.

My body's physical reaction to him wasn't good. It meant the one thing that I was trying to pretend it didn't mean.

That I was changing my stance on the one guy I wasn't supposed to care about.

That I had decided to hate for eternity.

And that scared me.

He was the enemy, and yet I couldn't bring myself to actually feel the anger that I'd forced myself to feel for so long.

It surprised me how quickly I could forget my previous feelings in favor of these new, blossoming feelings that had me completely out of sorts and confused.

And frustrated.

"Yep," I said quickly, popping the *p*.

"Good. I was worried I whacked your head too hard on the ground."

Confused, I glanced over at him. "What?"

His cheeks looked flushed as he waved in the direction of my tent. Then he glanced back at me, and a worried look passed over his face. "I helped you get into your tent last night. You were all cramped in the chair, and I was worried that you'd wake up with a horrible cramp." Then he furrowed his brow. "Do you not remember any of this?"

My lips fluttered as I tried to figure out what I was going to say in response. But the only thing that came to mind was to just shake my head.

"Yeah, you were pretty out of it," Ben said softly. I could hear the laughter in his voice as he busied himself with his fishing pole.

I swallowed as fear crept up inside of my throat. "Did I…" I winced and closed my eyes. "Did I say anything?"

"Like what?"

I peeked over at him. He didn't seem alarmed or scared. Which was a good sign. I hadn't inexplicably declared my love for him or something. Thank goodness.

"I don't know. You tell me," I said quietly, hoping he would be the one to fill in the gaps of my memory.

He shook his head. "Nothing that stood out. You just mumbled under your breath something about confetti cake and raspberry." He smiled as he squinted down at me. "I'm guessing gelato flavors?"

Whew. That I could handle. Anything that revealed my ridiculous thoughts about him was going to be harder to explain. "Oh, yeah." I forced a laugh. "I'm trying some new flavors." I settled back in my chair and took in a deep, cleansing breath.

The mystery of my morning had been solved, and even

though I'd love to go back in time to keep Ben from being the person to help me to bed, I was satisfied with how the evening went.

At least, I hadn't embarrassed myself more than I normally could.

"That's a good sign," he said.

I furrowed my brow as I glanced over at him. "What?"

He was silent for a moment as his gaze remained focused on the ocean. Then he shrugged. "That you're creating new flavors. It's a relief."

"A relief?" I wasn't sure how to read his cryptic words. *Relief, good sign.* Those were words a person used when they were concerned about someone. Was he worried about me like that? And if that was true, why?

He nodded. "Yeah." His gaze drifted to mine, and when his smile grew on his lips, I found my breath catching in my throat. I could feel his concern for me even though I was trying to ignore it.

Not sure how I was going to face any of this, I just swallowed—pushing down all the emotions that had risen up inside of me—and focused back on the ocean. If I could just keep my attention on fishing, I just might be able to survive this weekend. If Ben insisted on distracting me like he was, I wasn't sure how I was going to get out of this situation with my strength intact.

I heard Ben clear his throat, but I didn't move to look at him. Right now, I was confused, and I didn't like feeling that way. He needed to remain in his world, and I would remain in mine. In our separate corners, I would be safe.

It was when I came out, when I allowed him to pull me into conversation, that's when I felt confused.

When I risked the one thing I was sure I couldn't handle, at least, not right now.

I couldn't get hurt.

Not when I was sure it would break me.

I spent the morning eating a makeshift breakfast from my cooler of food. Some crackers with peanut butter and sunflower seeds. It wasn't your typical breakfast, but it was what I remembered eating with my grandfather. And for some reason, it felt as good as homemade pot roast with mashed potatoes.

That was the thing about memories. They had a way of completing me when I felt lonely. All I had to do was take a trip down memory lane, and suddenly, all my worries would fade away.

And that was what I needed right now.

I needed my confusion toward Ben to be masked with memories that made me happy. That made me feel complete.

Ben seemed busy as well, and it wasn't until mid-morning that I saw him stand and walk over to the taped line between us. I could feel his gaze on me once more.

And before I could stop myself, I turned to face him. Then I winced, realizing that my plan to pretend as if I didn't see him was now shot, because there was no way I could do that when I was so obviously staring at him right now.

I sucked in my breath and decided to just go along

with it. After all, it was probably better to face my problem—or at least this problem—right now, than have to face it later.

"What's up?" I asked. It felt good to take charge of our conversation. He was always the one asking me first. If I started this conversation, it would at least help me feel in control—for now.

He studied me for a moment and then a smile slowly spread across his lips. "I'm just wondering if you want to make another wager."

I eyed him. "Okay," I said slowly. I didn't mind the last one so much. And making a bet with Ben seemed fine enough. It would help pass the time. "What are the stakes?"

He chuckled as he slipped his hands into his front pockets again. "What's the one thing you want from me."

I inhaled, choking on my spit. I coughed a few times until the tickle in my throat subsided. I glanced up at him to see that his brows were furrowed. As if he were legitimately worried about me.

I raised my hand as I reached down, grabbed my water bottle, and took a sip. Once my coughing had calmed down, I turned to face him. "What I want from you?"

He nodded.

I sat back as I chewed on his question. There was a lot I wished I could change. I wanted to go back in time and make it so that his family never came to this island. I wanted my grandmother's business to stay intact.

Before I could stop myself, I blurted out, "You leaving

the island." Just as the words left my lips, I slapped my hand over my mouth and stared up at him.

His eyebrows were raised as he stared at me. Then he scoffed and glanced away. I watched him, hoping he wouldn't be too upset with what I said.

Did he hate me now?

A few seconds passed before he nodded and glanced back at me. "Okay. If you win, I'll leave."

The rock that sat in my stomach hardened as I took in his words. Sure, I'd responded that way because, for a moment, that's what I thought I wanted. I wasn't so sure anymore. But, not wanting to lose face, I just nodded.

"And if I win?" I asked. My response came out in a whisper.

He tsked. "It's going to be big. I mean, if you want me to leave the island, I get something equally as impressive, right?"

Heat was now permeating my cheeks; the ridiculousness of this conversation wasn't lost on me. What were we doing? What was he doing? Did we really think this was the wisest way to establish what we wanted?

But, I'd gone this far, I might as well finish it.

"Sure," I said as I nodded.

He pursed his lips together for a moment before he spoke. Then he said the next sentence very slowly, as if he wanted me to catch every word.

"One kiss."

7

I stared at him.

Was he serious?

He couldn't be serious.

This was a joke.

A mean, very weird joke.

In a moment, he was going to laugh and point at me as he confessed that he was just trying to get a rise out of me and that he couldn't believe I would be so gullible.

Because right now, with the way my heart was racing, I couldn't believe it either.

"A kiss?" I choked out. The words felt as strange to say as they did to hear.

He nodded.

"Wh-why?" Didn't he realize how bets worked? He was supposed to ask for something he actually wanted. We were enemies. He wasn't supposed to want to *kiss* me.

He scoffed, but then a moment later, his expression grew serious as he studied me.

My heart began to pound, and I was sure my cheeks were as red as the nail polish my grandmother always wore.

And that only angered me more. Here he was, making a joke at my expense. He'd proposed a kiss, and I was an idiot to think that he really meant it. I was an idiot to let his words affect me.

I hated myself sometimes.

"Har, har. Very funny," I said as I stood and moved toward the edge of the pier. Then I sat down, dangling my feet over the edge. I needed some distance from Ben. I was losing my mind when he was around. I was taking him seriously for some unknown reason, and in doing so, I was going to have my heart broken—shattered into a million pieces.

Something had happened between last night and this morning. Something had changed in how I felt for Ben, and I was rapidly losing control over the rational part of my mind.

He had sucked me in, and suddenly, I had no control over anything anymore.

Movement next to me startled me, and I jumped and turned to see Ben as he sat down next to me. His arm brushed mine, which sent shivers erupting across my skin.

Out of instinct, I reached up to grab hold of the place on my arm where his skin had touched mine and pull it closer to my body. I wasn't sure why, but I felt if I replaced the feeling of his touch with the feeling of my own hand, I could somehow forget what it felt like when he touched me.

Because that seemed to be the only thought going through my mind right now.

His touch. His proximity. All of it was assaulting my senses and confusing me.

"I wasn't joking," he said when he'd settled down next to me.

Fear clung to my chest as I turned to look at him. He *was* joking, and now he had taken it too far. Despite his insistence that he'd been serious, I knew he wasn't. It hurt that he was playing with my emotions like this.

In the end, I was going to break. Because no matter how I sliced it, there was no reason for him to actually execute this if he were to win. After all, why would he want to kiss me?

"You certainly commit," I said, hating that so much of my emotion was evident in my voice. I swallowed as I attempted to remove the hurt that was coursing through my chest.

He was taking this too far. I was beginning to believe that he wanted to kiss me, and that was just cruel.

"I like you, Scarlett," he said in a whoosh of air and words.

Everything around me stilled as his words settled around me. I blinked a few times as if I needed the reassurance that I was actually awake and not just dreaming all of this. But, after a quick and painful pinch to my leg, I realized this was really happening.

I was awake and Ben was sitting next to me, telling me that he liked me.

He blew out his breath as he rubbed his hands on his thighs. "I've liked you for a long time. Ever since we moved onto the island." He cleared his throat. "But I know how much my family has hurt you. I know you dislike me. And believe me, if I could take it back, I would."

I felt his gaze on me, and even though I wanted to look at him, I didn't. He was right. I was hurting. I was broken. Even though he didn't personally do anything *to* me, his family had, and that wasn't something I could easily forget —no matter that there might be a part of me that wanted to.

"I just think if you could see me as someone else, someone other than a person who crushed your family's dreams, I might have a chance."

Tears stung my eyes, but I wasn't going to let them fall. I was going to be strong. Sure, I didn't know how I felt about his declaration, but there was no way I was going to give him hope.

Not until I had time to digest his words.

I turned to focus on him. Even though I'd allowed myself to have a momentary lapse in judgement, I still had a chance to save my gelato shop. If he left the island— taking Sam's Ice Cream Shop with him, I could save Mama Schmidt's Gelato.

"Will you take Sam's with you?" I asked, holding his gaze so he could feel how serious I was.

Ben studied me for a moment, his brow furrowed. "Your part of the bet." Then he held my gaze. "Is that what you want?"

I wasn't proud about how I was acting, but I also knew that if I didn't take this chance now, I might regret it. And I was tired of regrets.

"Yes." I stilled my expression as I studied him. "If you promise that you'll take Sam's and leave Magnolia, then I agree to your terms."

He furrowed his brow again. "You'll kiss me if I win?"

Out of instinct, my gaze dropped to his lips. My entire body heated at the thought of what it might feel like to press my own lips to his. An ache rose up inside of me. One that mixed the desire to have him leave Magnolia with the desire to feel his arms wrapped around me and his lips pressed to mine.

It was a strange sensation. Like feeling hot and cold at the same time. My body didn't know what to think—what to do. I felt frozen to the spot. Pain and anguish filled my soul and left me feeling incomplete.

I was being pulled in two different directions, and I wasn't sure what to listen to. If he won, I would kiss him, and all the emotions that I'd tried to dam up would break free. Because if he won, Sam's would stay and Mama Schmidt's Gelato would shut down.

But if I won, Sam's would leave. My family's legacy might have a fighting chance to survive. But that would come at a cost. Because, in the end, I would be left just as alone as I was right now.

If I won, Ben would leave. And that thought ached more than anything else right now.

Remembering that he'd asked me a question, I turned to nod. Then I extended my hand. "If you win, I'll kiss you."

A small, almost shy smile spread across Ben's lips, and my heart picked up speed. Warmth exploded up my arm and throughout my body as he slipped his hand into mine and we shook on it. Then he dropped my hand and turned back to the ocean.

It felt like an eternity passed before he sighed and moved to stand. "Well, looks like I've got a competition to win," he said as he gave me a wink and headed back to his spot on the pier.

Not wanting to think about Ben, his lips, or the way his wink sent butterflies dive-bombing my stomach, I hurried to stand as well.

"Um, me too," I mumbled as I hurried over to my pole. I jerked the line a few times and then decided to just reel in my lure and start over again.

Ben seemed completely dedicated to winning this bet. I spent the whole afternoon fishing alongside him, but he never looked up to speak to me. Instead, he kept his face focused on the ocean and his pole.

I was beginning to sweat—not only from the heat of the sun overhead, but from the anticipation of what was going to happen. My lips felt dry, so I licked them, and when that didn't do the trick, I opened my cooler and found my last water bottle. After cracking it open and taking a sip, my phone chimed.

I set my water down and glanced down at my screen.

It was a text from Maggie.

Maggie: How are things going? Catching a lot?

I smiled as I squinted against the sunlight and texted her back.

Me: Great. Trying to catch something. Gotta win.

Maggie: Need some lunch? Clem and I were thinking about stopping by.

Yes. I needed that. I needed a break from Ben, fishing, and my confusing thoughts. If I were around my friends, they might be able to help me sort through my feelings. The ones that I couldn't figure out no matter how much I tried to process them.

Me: Yes, please!

Maggie: 😊 All right, we'll be there in thirty.

I sent her a thumbs-up emoji and then tucked my phone into the cupholder of my chair. I leaned back, blowing out my breath as I tipped my face toward the sky and, closing my eyes, took in a deep breath.

My thoughts roamed over the events of the day. From my conversation with Ben to the few measly fish I'd caught. None of which were going to win me anything. Ben had some success as well, but nothing that would clinch a victory for him either.

Which I was relieved about.

Or not.

I was still trying to figure that piece out.

True to her word, Maggie arrived with Clementine thirty minutes after our last text. I'd lost myself in a Netflix show on my phone when I heard their footsteps on the pier.

Ready to eat and take a break from sitting next to Ben and not talking—only obsessing—I leapt to my feet with a grin on my face. I hurried over to them, and from the corner of my eye, I saw Ben do the same. He was smiling in the way that made my heart pitter-patter as he joined up with me.

He shook Maggie and Clementine's hands and asked them how they were doing. After the pleasantries were over, Maggie handed one of the food bags over to Ben, telling him she'd brought him lunch. He thanked her and then glanced over at me.

"We're going to eat at the tables," I said, nodding in the direction of the picnic area at the end of the pier.

"Oh," he said as he held the top of his bag closed and then nodded over to his chair. "I guess I'll go settle in. Thanks again, Maggie."

She nodded and I moved to usher them down the pier.

"Hang on," I said as I reached out to grab Ben's arm before he left. My fingers lingered on his skin, and the sensation sent jolts of electricity throughout my body. It took a moment for my brain to catch up, and once it did, I dropped my hand like I'd been burned.

Ben glanced down at where I'd touched him and then back up to meet my gaze. "Yeah?" he asked.

I pinched my lips together as I attempted to calm my reaction before I spoke. When I was sure I had a handle on it, I cleared my throat and nodded toward my pole. "Do you mind keeping an eye on that for me?"

He followed my gesture and then glanced back down at me. His eyebrows rose, and I could tell that he wanted to make a joke, but he just nodded.

"Yeah, sure. I can do that."

I smiled at him and then made my way back over to Maggie and Clem. "Thanks! I'll be back in about an hour."

He gave me a quick salute, but before he could say anything more, I joined up with Maggie and Clem and we walked down the pier and over to the picnic tables.

As we sat down and opened up the lobster rolls that Maggie had grabbed, I sighed. It was good to get some space from Ben. If anything, it meant I was going to be able to actually think.

I needed a break from the emotions that arose every time he was around.

I'd started out this competition with one goal in mind, and yet, somehow, that goal had managed to change. Now, I wasn't sure what I wanted. The only thing I knew was, I was never going to be the same.

Things had changed between Ben and I, and right now, the best way to deal with it was to ignore it.

I'd face it later.

For now, it wasn't going to exist.

8

After we devoured our lunch, I stretched my legs out on the bench and leaned back on my arms. The feeling of a full stomach mixed with the warmth of the sun's rays gave me a feeling of satisfaction that I'd been craving the last few hours.

Right now, I had no worries. Right now, I could just be. There was no gelato shop to save and no Ben to confuse me.

Life was better when I ignored all my worries.

"So how's the competition going?" Clementine asked.

I peeked over at her and then tipped my face to the sky again. "It's going. Not much in terms of anything that could clinch the victory for me, but there's still time."

As the words spilled from my lips, I felt confused. I was normally excited to talk about fishing—or even think about it—but right now, I wasn't feeling it. Fishing just brought on confusing emotions about the shop mixed with Ben and his proposal.

I wasn't sure if I wanted him to actually leave, and I was equally unsure if I wanted to kiss him.

Either way, I wasn't sure which one I could count a win and which I could count as a loss.

I was a jumbled mix of confusion.

Clementine nodded. "That's good. And you've got Ben to keep you company," she said slowly.

There was a tone to her voice that confused me. I glanced up at her to see her studying me.

"Yeah."

"Am I missing something?" Maggie asked.

Clementine glanced over at her. "Ben's family brought a rival ice cream shop to the island. It was hard on Scar's family."

Maggie glanced over at me, and I nodded. She furrowed her brow. "I'm sorry. He seems so nice."

I winced at her words. The truth was, he was nice. Ben was really nice. The more time I spent around him, the more my previous notions about him were breaking down. Which left me confused and unsure of anything anymore.

"Oh, Ben's the greatest," Clementine said. "It just makes for a sordid history."

"So, have things been weird?" Maggie asked.

I tucked my legs back under the table and sighed as I leaned forward and rested my forehead in the crook of my arm in front of me.

"It's gotten…complicated."

"How?" Clementine asked.

I glanced up to see both women studying me.

I took in a deep breath and held it for a moment before I slowly let it out. "We made a bet."

Clementine leaned forward and propped her face up in her hands as she studied me. "What kind of bet?" she asked as she wiggled her eyebrows.

"Not that kind of bet," I said quickly before the memory of exactly what I had agreed to came over me. "Or maybe it is," I said feeling even more confused than I had earlier.

"What?" Maggie asked as she leaned in.

I decided it was best to tell them what had happened. I didn't hold back. I went through every detail of what had happened between Ben and I ever since he walked back into my life less than twenty-four hours ago.

I ended with them coming down the pier. My words lingered in the air as I sat back and watched to see what their reaction would be. Maggie was staring at the tabletop and Clementine was staring straight at me.

"So, if you win, Ben has to leave, and if Ben wins, you have to kiss him?" Clementine asked.

I nodded. Man, saying those words out loud made us sound crazy. "Yes. That's the bet."

Clementine leaned back. "Wow. I mean, you really laid it all out on the line with telling him he'd have to leave. And his response to that was to ask for a kiss? That seems super risky for him."

Maggie shook her head. "I don't think so. You said he doesn't really want to run the family business and that he's liked you forever. To me, it sounds like, either way, he's getting what he wants." She eyed me. "How do you feel about the terms? I mean, I know you'll like it if you win, but what if you lose?"

My stomach lightened and the ridiculous butterflies that lived there decided it was time to take flight again. I sucked in my breath as I shrugged. "I don't know."

"Ooo, I think that's a yes, she does want to kiss him," Clementine said as a mischievous expression passed over her face.

My first instinct was to protect myself. There was no way I wanted to admit to any of what Clementine was saying. Even though part of me agreed with her, the sane part of me—the part that wanted to protect me until the end of time—fought against it.

"I do not. I just…" I wasn't sure how I'd planned on finishing that sentence. If I didn't want to kiss him, why did it feel like I did?

Maggie sighed as she studied me. "I think the question is, do you want him to leave that bad? If you're having confusing thoughts about kissing him, how are you going to feel if you run him off the island? I mean, once he's gone, he'll be gone. I doubt a guy could come back from something like that."

"Ooo, you're right. Once you not only reject his kiss but push him out of here, I doubt Ben will come running back to you," Clementine said as she nodded at Maggie.

My stomach lurched, and suddenly, my delicious lunch felt as if it were going to make a reappearance. I swallowed hard as I tried to figure out what my problem was. How I had let things get so wonky was beyond me.

I was a level-headed girl. I rarely let my emotions dictate my actions. But somehow, during this entire experience, I'd let things get out of control. And I wasn't sure how I was going to fix it.

Where did I even start?

"We're not trying to confuse you," Maggie said as she reached across the table and patted my hand.

I offered her a weak smile and nodded. I knew they only had in mind what was best for me, but that didn't change the fact that I felt lost.

I'd stoked my family's anger toward the Williams for so long, and I was only beginning to realize that, perhaps, I didn't hate them. And not only that, I wasn't sure if I wanted to.

"I guess the good news is, you still have some time. I mean, the competition is over, what, tomorrow? Maybe take tonight to figure out what you really want." Maggie offered me a smile, and I had to say, I was grateful for it. I needed that boost.

"Thanks," I said.

Clementine popped into my line of sight. "I'm here too. Text me whenever. With Dad gone and Maggie stealing my brother, I'm preeetty bored."

I laughed as I stretched my arms up to the sky and curved my back, which helped lessen the stress I felt in my muscles. It felt good, chatting with these ladies. They helped bring my situation into focus.

"I'll do that," I said as I dropped my arms to my side and let out my breath. "I should get back. The competition isn't going to win itself."

Maggie and Clementine nodded, and we all stood up from the table. After a quick goodbye, I turned and made my way down the pier. As I did, a huge commotion drew my attention over. A crowd had gathered around my taped-off section. I could hear cheers and conversations as I pushed against the throng.

Something had been caught, and from the cheers, it was big.

My heart began to pound in my chest as I neared, and when I burst through the throng of people, my head felt as if it were spinning. Ben had my pole in one hand, and inside of the net thrashed a bluefish.

A *massive* bluefish.

From the look of its length, from head to tail, it was the biggest one I'd ever seen.

"Wh-what happened?" I managed out as I stepped up to Ben.

He glanced down at me as he handed the net over. I took it but then quickly had to shift my body to account for the weight. This fish had to be at least fifty pounds.

"You caught this," he said as he smiled down at me.

I stared at him, not quite sure what to say. He studied me for a moment and then gave me a wink.

"Say something to your fans." He dipped closer to my ear.

I shivered as his warm breath and the feeling of his lips so close to my skin washed over me. I knew he's said something, I was just having a hard time remembering what that was.

"My fans?" I breathed out. I felt so out of sorts that I needed him to break it down for me. If this fish meant what I thought it did, I was pretty much the winner of this competition. Which also meant I'd won our bet.

Ben was going to leave.

Cue the ache inside my stomach. It made me feel nauseous, and even though I knew I should be happy, I wasn't. The matching ache inside my heart told me I wasn't sure it was a victory anymore.

Ben leaving Magnolia wasn't the trophy I wanted.

Ben chuckled as he extended his hand and motioned to the people who had gathered around to see the fish. "Give them some encouraging words. Something." He smiled down at me and then leaned in again. His proximity was sending ripples of pleasure across my skin. "You've pretty much won this thing, Scar. If you don't say something, people are just going to give up."

Through the cloud of haze as my body responded to his nearness, I nodded and focused my attention. Then I cleared my throat and spoke. I could do this. It was easy to say *something*. Right?

Luckily, my grandfather's ability to spin a good line was

passed down to me, and I managed to pull myself together. I told the crowd I hoped they had the same fortune as me and to keep the spirit of competition alive by beating me.

Everyone laughed, and not too long after I finished, they all dispersed to their prospective spots.

Now alone, I let out my breath as I dropped down onto my chair. My nerves were ragged and my muscles were tense. I needed the release that sitting gave me.

Norman, the city councilman over this competition, came to gather the fish from me. He tagged it and told me it would be stored on ice until tomorrow morning when they would weigh the final catches and pronounce the winner.

I nodded and watched him for a moment as he carried my fish down the pier. I collapsed back against my chair and allowed my mind to settle for a moment. The realization that I just might have caught the biggest fish of the competition washed over me.

It was as if all the things I'd thought I wanted were coming true…so why didn't I feel happier?

Movement over in Ben's spot drew my attention over. He was busy reeling in his pole, and instead of casting it again, he removed his hook and began to put his pole away. I parted my lips, confused as I watched his movements.

It didn't look like he was planning on casting his line again. No, from the way he was packing his belongings into his backpack, it looked as if he were…leaving.

"What's up?" I asked before I stopped myself. I'd leapt

from my chair and crossed the taped divide between us. I shoved my hands into my front pockets as I glanced up at him, hoping I looked curious and not creepy.

Ben studied me for a moment before he smiled and shrugged. "I figure it's time to head back. After all, I doubt I'll be able to catch anything bigger than that fish." He nodded in the direction that Norman had gone.

I followed his gesture with my gaze. I felt so confused. Any other time, I would have been celebrating the fact that he was leaving. But now? Now I didn't feel happy.

I felt sad.

"Do you really have to go? I mean, you could at least stay to witness my victory in person." I laughed as I reached out and play-punched his shoulder.

He raised his eyebrows and dropped his gaze down to his arm. Heat permeated my cheeks as I cleared my throat and covered my fist with my other hand.

Who was I turning into? Who was this person? It certainly wasn't anyone I recognized.

I wasn't sure what was going on, but I did know one thing, I didn't want him to leave. Not until I figured out how I felt about him. About us.

Us.

Ugh. Why did my heart flutter at that word? Why did my body begin to warm when I thought about him? Why couldn't I remember what it felt like to hate him?

What had once been a roaring fire of anger was now barely a flicker of light. I was pretty sure that it had burned down to embers by now.

I was confused about a lot of things, but one thing had become apparent. I didn't hate Ben anymore, and the last thing I wanted was to run him out of town.

"Ben, listen, I—"

"We had a deal, and I'm a man of my word," he said as he folded his chair up and stuffed it into his over-the-shoulder bag. "Let's not get distracted by anything other than our plan." He gathered up his final items and then turned to face me.

My lips were parted. I wanted to say something—anything—to get him to stay, but I could tell from the determined look in his eye, he didn't want to hear it. And the doubt and fear that my desires would make a difference to him rose up inside of me.

How could I ask him to stay when it was so apparent for so long that I'd wanted him to leave?

Changing decision like that didn't seem fair to him, and the last thing I wanted to do was hurt him. Not when I was so embarrassed by how I'd treated him in the past.

Ben studied me for a moment before he smiled and ran his hand through his hair. "I should go." He stepped forward but paused as he looked down at me. "Good luck, Scarlett. I mean it." His last few words drifted off as he stayed next to me for a few seconds more, and then walked past.

I tipped my face toward him, but before I could say anything, he was gone. Down the pier, over to his truck. I watched as he pulled away.

Now alone, I glanced around. I brought my hand up to

my other arm and rubbed it a few times as I tried to gain control of my emotions. It was late afternoon. The sun was no longer high in the sky. It was on its way down to the horizon. I watched as its light reflected off the water.

Taking in a deep breath, I sat back down on my chair.

Ben wanted to go, and who was I to stop him? If he wanted to leave, I was pretty sure there was nothing I could say that would deter him. He seemed determined to walk out the door. If I tried to hold him back, he would still leave.

And I would be left alone, heartbroken with no one else to blame but myself.

Taking in a deep breath, I tipped my head back on my chair and closed my eyes.

I should be happy. This was what I'd wanted. Ben was gone, and he was taking Sam's with him. This is what I had been looking forward to, and now that it was happening, I should be grateful.

Except, no amount of convincing myself to feel happy about any of this was actually working.

No matter how I sliced it, Ben was gone. And I was alone once more.

Somehow, during these last twenty four hours with Ben, my anger had turned to something else

And I was pretty sure that something else was the opposite of hate.

9

I hadn't realized how accustomed I'd grown to having Ben next to me until he was gone. Now alone, I spent the aching minutes and hours staring out at the ocean. I didn't feel like fishing, but I also didn't feel like leaving.

What did I have to go back to?

An empty apartment and a failing gelato shop.

If anything, it was just going to be yet another physical representation of the failure that was my life. Growing up, I'd had dreams, and yet somehow, none of those dreams seemed to have been realized.

Instead, I was a failing business owner who was pretty sure she was going to die alone. I might as well buy a hoard of cats and really lean into it.

"Finished fishing?" A deep voice asked from behind me.

I turned to see Bert standing behind me. He was grinning as he nodded toward my pole. It was tucked into the holder with the hook fastened to one of the eyes of the pole. I guess in my depression from Ben leaving, I'd completely forgotten what I was doing and hadn't cast it back into the ocean.

Not wanting to get into the nuances of my life, I just smiled and shook my head. "Nah. It's not like I can beat the big mama I caught earlier." I waved in the direction that Norman had gone.

Bert followed my gesture and then peeked back at me. I could tell that he wanted to say something, but he was holding back.

And that intrigued me.

For all the years that I'd known Bert, I hadn't taken him to be a secretive man. He was a shoot-from-the-hip kind of guy. So the fact that he was very obviously chewing on something had me on high alert.

"It's best to just spit it out," I said as I shielded my eyes so I could look up at him.

He studied me for a moment before he shoved his hands into his front pockets and cleared his throat. "It's just that I think Ben might have switched poles when he reeled that sucker up." His voice drifted off as I stared at him.

"I'm sorry, what?" I asked. My mind was trying to piece together what he said. His words felt like a 1000-piece puzzle without the box art to guide me.

Bert cleared his throat again. "Earlier, when he reeled in the fish. I think it was on his line originally."

I was pretty sure my eyebrows had joined my hairline by now. With every word he spoke, realization dawned on me.

Ben had lied? Why?

"Wait, so you saw him reel the fish in with his pole?"

Bert nodded. "I think so. I mean, I was just passing by, but it wasn't that pole. I'd know that pole anywhere."

He pointed to my grandfather's pole that I'd brought for good luck. I studied it and then glanced back at him. "So he lied?"

Bert studied me. "I don't know, but…I'm pretty sure," he said with a nod of his head that caused his floppy white hair to jostle.

I swallowed as I dropped my gaze. My mind was spinning as anger and frustration coursed through me. Ben had given me his win? Why? Did he have that little respect for me?

Why did he think I needed a helping hand?

And why had he given up on trying to win?

I stood and grabbed my backpack. There was no way I was going to let him leave the island like that. I was going to find him, and I was going to confront him.

"I'll be back," I said to Bert. "Tell Norman I'm leaving for a few hours."

Bert nodded, but I didn't stick around to see if he had anything more to say. I was on my way to find Ben and nothing was going to stop me.

Just as I climbed into my truck, I shot Maggie a text to see if Ben had shown up at Magnolia Inn. Thankfully, she was quick to respond, saying she'd been about to text me. She wanted to know what had happened to cause him to come back early.

With the confirmation set squarely in my mind, I made my way to Magnolia Inn. All the way there, I played what I was going to say to him over and over in my mind.

I was hurt. I was angry. And more still, I was upset that I cared enough to be hurt and angry. He'd cheated me out of a real win, and at the same time, he'd completely given up on the bet we'd established.

I pulled into the parking lot and turned off my truck. I took in a deep breath as my fingers lingered on the door handle. The ridiculous butterflies in my stomach decided to come to life, and suddenly, everything I'd worked up in my mind flew out and I couldn't remember what I was doing or what I had planned to say.

Realizing that I couldn't spend the day holed up in my truck, I decided to throw caution to the wind. I'd figure out what I was going to say when I got there. I was an intelligent woman; my plan would come back to me.

I had to believe that.

As soon as I pulled open the front doors of Magnolia Inn and stepped inside, Maggie appeared in front of me. She had on an apron that was covered with flour. Whatever she had been making must have exploded on her because she had specks of flour dusting her cheeks.

"What happened? Is the competition over?" she asked as she ran her gaze over me. Her eyebrows were drawn together.

I shook my head. "I'm not sure. That's why I have to talk to Ben. Where is he?"

She glanced around and then back at me. "I think he's outside on the patio. Archer was laying brick for a new bonfire pit, and last I saw, Ben was headed in that direction."

I nodded and sidestepped her. Just as I passed by, I paused and glanced back at her. "Get any flour in the bowl, Mags?" I asked.

She laughed and waved me away. "Har har. Hey, I never said I was an amazing baker. I'm trying."

I chuckled as I walked toward the back door of the inn. It was nice to have Maggie as a buffer. She helped relax me, which helped me prep for the conversation I was about to have. I still couldn't remember what I was going to say, but I felt happier. Less stressed.

And right now, I needed that.

When I got out to the patio, I looked around and located Ben, but not Archer. That helped me feel better. The last thing I needed was for Archer to be privy to our conversation—or whatever words were going to spill from my lips.

I wanted Ben, and only Ben, to know what I was about to say. This was a small town, and although I knew Maggie and Archer could keep a secret, I still wanted to keep my freak-out session to the least amount of people possible.

Ben was sitting at a picnic table, facing the ocean. He was staring out at the water as I approached. I held my breath when I neared him, not sure if I should say something or just sit down.

Before I could decide, his gaze drifted over to me and he startled.

"Geez," he said as he closed his eyes and gripped his shirt over his heart. "You scared the crap out of me." He peered up at me with a confused expression. "What are you doing here?"

Gathering my courage, I plopped down on the bench next to him. I misjudged the distance between us and, in the process, brushed my arm against his. Shivers erupted across my skin, and out of instinct, I sucked in my breath. Touching him felt so…normal. And right. The warmth that was now rushing through my body left me feeling listless and at ease.

It was so strange.

I wanted to test it again.

"Hold still," I said.

Ben had his arms resting on the tabletop in front of him. His hands were clasped together. I raised my fingers and brushed them against his skin. I could feel the goosebumps my touch instigated. It was the same reaction I was having.

"What are you doing?" Ben asked, his voice deepening.

The depth of his tone caused my breath to catch in my throat. The butterflies inside of my stomach were now dive-bombing all over the place. There was no denying it anymore, I liked Ben.

I liked Ben Williams.

I raised my gaze up to meet his, and all of the thoughts I'd had before of chewing him out left my mind. All I could think about was how he was now centimeters away from me. If I wanted to, all I had to do was lean in and press my lips to his.

I could feel his gaze on me. I could feel his confusion as I searched his soul. He was hurting, I could see that. And all I could think about was taking that pain away.

So I leaned in and brushed my lips against his. The kiss was soft and barely lasted a second before he pulled back.

"What are you doing?" he asked. His eyebrows were drawn together, and his eyes were searching my face and my gaze as if the answer were written there.

I held his gaze and then slowly smiled. "I'm a woman of my word," I said softly.

Ben furrowed his brown and then sighed as he dropped his gaze. "Who told you?"

"Bert."

"Bert," he said quietly. "I should have known."

Needing to know why he did what he did, I dipped down so that I could meet his gaze. "Why did you say I caught the fish when you did?"

He studied me for a moment before he reached up and tucked my hair behind my ear. My whole body warmed from the feeling of his fingertips lingering on my cheek and then trailing down to my jawbone.

"Even though I wanted that kiss, I wanted you to win more." He brought his gaze up to meet mine, and just as he did, he cupped my cheek with his hand and ran his thumb across my bottom lip.

The world around me began to fade away, and I couldn't stop myself from leaning into him. I wanted to feel his body next to mine. I never wanted him to leave.

I closed my eyes for a moment and then opened them back up, allowing my feelings to permeate the air between us. He needed to know how I felt.

"Why are you being so nice to me?" I asked.

His other hand found my arm, and he brushed his fingertips across my skin, causing goosebumps to rise up. When my gaze met his again, my breath caught in my throat.

I could feel his affection for me as he held my gaze hostage in his. He leaned forward and rested his forehead on mine.

"Because I love you," he said softly.

I closed my eyes as his words filled every broken crack inside of me. That was exactly what I needed to hear. It had been missing in my life, and yet, it had been here all along.

"You do?" I asked. There was a part of me that feared he'd take it back. Or that I had heard incorrectly.

Before he answered, I felt his fingertips on my chin, and he gently guided my face upward until he was studying me again. Then he leaned forward and brushed his lips against mine.

This time, neither of us pulled away. Instead, I

wrapped my arms around his neck, and he wrapped his hands around my waist and pulled until I was next to him.

Our breaths matched. Our heartbeats collided as we held each other. Our lips synced, and as I parted my lips so he could deepen the kiss, all my fear and worry slipped away.

This was what I needed. This was what I wanted. I just needed to get out of my way long enough to allow it.

I'd found the person I was meant to be with. Sure, he wasn't the guy I'd pictured, and I'd been sure there was no way Ben and I could be anything more than enemies, but for the first time in my life, I was happy to be wrong.

We eventually broke apart. Our breaths heavy yet calm. Ben grinned over at me as he wrapped his hand around mine and pulled it onto his lap. I leaned my head on his shoulder as we stared out at the ocean.

"Forgive me?"

I tipped my face up to study him. "For what?"

He squeezed my hand. "For being a dork. For leaving. And for lying to you about the fish."

"Oh. For that." I took in a deep breath and then slowly nodded. "I think I can do that."

Ben laughed, and I loved the sound of its rumble in his chest. I reached up and pressed my lips to his cheek.

"Promise not to leave?"

He glanced down at me. "What about our bet?"

I shrugged. "I'm still the winner. I think for five grand I can forgive you and call it even."

He nodded, and I settled back down on his shoulder. "You have yourself a deal."

We spent the rest of the evening sitting at the picnic table, watching the sunset. The world around us stilled, and for the first time in a long time, I felt peace.

I felt as if this was where I belonged. And no matter what the future brought, I was sure I could handle it.

With Ben by my side, I could do anything.

I was finally whole.

***

The Inn on Harmony Island

I'm also SO excited to announce that Abigail and company star in their own series based on Harmony Island. You'll reconnect with all the friends you read about in this series, but discover new move-ins and new stories—and oh-so-swoon-worthy romances.

Grab the first book in the series, The Inn on Harmony Island to make sure you don't miss out HERE!

Want more Red Stiletto Bookclub Romances?? Head on over and grab you next read HERE.

For a full reading order of Anne-Marie's books, you can find them HERE.

Or scan below:

Printed in Great Britain
by Amazon